To Michèle

Groundwood Books / Douglas & McIntyre
720 Bathurst Street, Suite 500, Toronto, Ontario M5S 2R4
Distributed in the U.S.A. by Publishers Group West
1700 Fourth Street, Berkeley, CA 94710

We acknowledge for their financial support of our publishing program the Canada Council for the Arts, the Ontario Arts Council and the Government of Canada through the Book Publishing Industry Development Program (BPIDP).

ONTARIO ARTS COUNCIL
CONSEIL DES ARTS DE L'ONTARIO

National Library of Canada Cataloguing in Publication
Gay, Marie-Louise
Good Morning Sam / Marie-Louise Gay
ISBN 0-88899-528-8
I. Title.
PS8563.A868G66 2003   jC813'.54   C2002-902935-X
PZ7

Library of Congress Control Number: 2002108235

Printed and bound in China

GOOD MORNING
SAM

MARIE-LOUISE GAY

A GROUNDWOOD BOOK DOUGLAS & McINTYRE TORONTO VANCOUVER BERKELEY

"Sam," called Stella. "Wake up!"

"I'm awake," yawned Sam. "I think."

"I'll help you get dressed," said Stella.
"No," said Sam. "I can do it by myself."

"Are you sure?"
"Yes," said Sam.

"Hurry up, then," said Stella.

"I'm hurrying," said Sam.

"Stella, help!" called Sam.
"My head grew bigger in the night."

"No, it didn't," said Stella.
"Ouf!" said Sam.

"Stella!" called Sam. "I can't find my underpants."
"Did you look in the bottom drawer?" asked Stella.
"I'm looking," said Sam.

"Sam," said Stella. "Are you in there?"
"Yes," answered Sam.

"Stella, help!" called Sam.
"I can't see. Did you turn off the lights?"

"No, I didn't," said Stella. "See?"
"Ouf!" said Sam.

"Stella! My sock has disappeared!"

"No, it didn't," said Stella. "Here it comes."

"Stella! Now my shoes are lost!
"Have you looked everywhere, Sam?"

"Yes," said Sam.
"Did you look in the closet?" asked Stella.

"Help!" cried Sam. "I can't get out."

"Sam? Are you in there?"
"No," said Sam.

"Stella, I'm ready! And I did it all by myself!"

"Didn't you forget something, Sam?"
"Oh," said Sam. "My pants!"

"Ta-daa!" sang Sam. "I'm really ready now."
"Finally," said Stella. "Let's go."

"Stella?" said Sam.
"What now?" sighed Stella.

"Didn't you forget something?" giggled Sam.